4/02

D1123106

For Michael Stearns, Prince of Editors
—B. C.

For Bunny, Robbie, and Ben,
and for Mary, the Queen of Ladybugs
—J. C.

The Prince of Butterflies was originally published, in a slightly different form,
by Disney Magazine Publishing, Inc., in *Disney's Big Time*, May 1995.

www.harcourt.com

Library of Congress Cataloging-in-Publication Data
Coville, Bruce.
The prince of butterflies/by Bruce Coville; illustrated by John Clapp.
p.   cm.
Summary: When surrounded by thousands of butterflies, eleven-year-old John
becomes transformed into one of them and finds his entire life altered because of this experience.
[1. Monarch butterfly—Fiction.   2. Butterflies—Fiction.]   I. Clapp, John, ill.   II. Title.
PZ7.C8344Pr   2002
[E]—dc21   99-50811
ISBN 0-15-201454-3

First edition
A C E G H F D B

Manufactured in China

The illustrations in this book were done in watercolor on Arches cold-press watercolor paper.
The display type was set in Nicholas Cochin.
The text type was set in Cochin.
Color separations by Bright Arts Ltd., Hong Kong
Manufactured by South China Printing Company, Ltd., China
This book was printed on totally chlorine-free Nymolla Matte Art paper.
Production supervision by Sandra Grebenar and Ginger Boyer
Designed by Linda Lockowitz

Although John Farrington isn't real, the plight of the monarchs is.
Ongoing habitat loss across North America keeps the species in danger of extinction.
—B. C.

THE *Prince* OF *Butterflies*

BRUCE COVILLE

Illustrations by
JOHN CLAPP

HARCOURT, INC.

San Diego   New York   London

Two days after John Farrington's eleventh birthday, a migration of monarch butterflies landed on his house.

When John came out the front door that morning, the monarchs covered the side of his home like some living carpet, their orange wings folding and unfolding so that the pattern never stayed the same from one moment to the next. Clusters of them decorated the porch railing, the lawn chairs, the family car, and patches of the side yard.

It was the most beautiful thing he had ever seen.

John made not a sound, for fear of frightening the butterflies away. And though his hands fairly itched to catch one, he worried that if he tried, the whole flock would take wing. Barely daring to breathe, he walked a few feet from the house then sank gently to the ground, where he held as still as he could.

This sitting still was not easy for John. He was rambunctious by nature, and preferred running and shouting to being quiet. But in this case he was willing to make an exception.

His self-control was rewarded when one of the butterflies landed on the toe of his sneaker. It opened and closed its wings once, then began to walk up his leg.

More butterflies started in John's direction, some simply turning so they were facing him, others fluttering toward him in short hops. Three landed on his left shoulder. One, particularly bold, came feather soft to his hand.

John swallowed nervously, trying to fight down a moment of fear. What could be more harmless than a butterfly? Yet he sensed something uncanny moving about him, something unnatural—or at least not *natural* as he understood the word. And then...

The butterflies spoke to him, a thousand voices whispering in his mind as delicately as a wing brushing his cheek. What they said— not in words but quite clearly nevertheless—was *Help!*

Panic shivered down John's spine, and it was all he could do to keep from leaping up and running away. Forcing himself to hold still, he closed his eyes and thought, *How? Why?*

More butterflies landed on his unmoving body, butterflies on his arms and legs, on his shoulders. Delicate creatures, fragile and . . . frightened. As they came to him, the image of a meadow, green and quiet, filled his mind.

We've lost the path, they whispered.

What path? thought John.

The butterfly road that we follow home. We have a green place near here

*where we stop to feed and rest. But we can't find it. Once there was so much
green. Where does it go?*

John recognized the meadow, for he had often played there
himself, until a construction company began turning it into a mini-
mall last September. Without intending to, he formed an image of
the meadow as it looked now.

Their despair washed over him like a wave.

What shall we do? That was the last haven we knew of on this part of the path. Where can we go now?

The question was asked by thousands of the butterflies. Under it drifted the sad thoughts of others who simply sighed with a sense of doom. Above it, clear and strong, rose a single bright voice that said, *Help us!*

Fear and wonder fought for control of John's soul. *What can I do?*

Is there another green place? Somewhere not too far away?

John remembered a day earlier that month when he had gone out to sell magazines for the school's playground fund. He had ridden his bike too far and gotten lost. He'd seen a meadow then that might do, an island of green still untouched by bulldozers.

When he formed an image of it in his mind, the butterflies rustled with excitement and relief. *Take us there!*

How?

Their answer came not in words, or pictures, or feelings, but
something stronger. The butterflies surrounded John, brushing
him with their wings, dropping their tiny scales on his eyes, his
arms, his legs...his two legs, four legs, six legs.

Stretching the unexpected wings that arched from his sides, John took flight.

His heart nearly burst with the joy of gliding through the warm air. Floating on the caress of soft breezes while ten thousand of his kind, flickering bright, flashing orange and black, fluttered all about him, he felt *not* alone in a way he never had before.

Lead us to the meadow, pleaded the flock.

Flapping his delicate wings, John flew up and away from his home until he could see the road he needed to follow. He fluttered along the side of it, guiding the monarchs above the houses.

They journeyed through the morning, settling now on a hedge, now on a tree. *Just a little farther,* he kept promising. *Just a little farther.*

When at last they reached the meadow, the butterflies settled to its weedy wildness with a sense of joyous relief that lifted him as if it were a warm wind.

John spent the morning with the butterflies, crawling along slender green stems, unrolling his long tube of a tongue to sip sweet nectar, luxuriating in the feel of the sun on his wings.

Then, at noon, with the sun straight overhead, he suddenly realized he was in trouble.

Can you turn me back? he asked frantically. *My mother is going to be furious with me for not telling her where I was going.*

Stay, whispered the butterflies. *Stay with us.*

John felt the sun on his wings, wings that could lift him to the sky, carry him free and far, and he longed to remain a butterfly. But he thought of his parents, and how they would fear for him, would miss him.

He thought of how he would miss them.

I can't, he told the butterflies sadly. *I have to go home.*

They gathered above him, and in a moment it was finished. Like a butterfly turning back to a caterpillar, he lost his wings and was a boy once more, blinking in the sunlight.

His feet were blistered by the time he got home, and he was indeed in trouble. But he didn't really mind; he would trade a week of being grounded for a day with wings anytime.

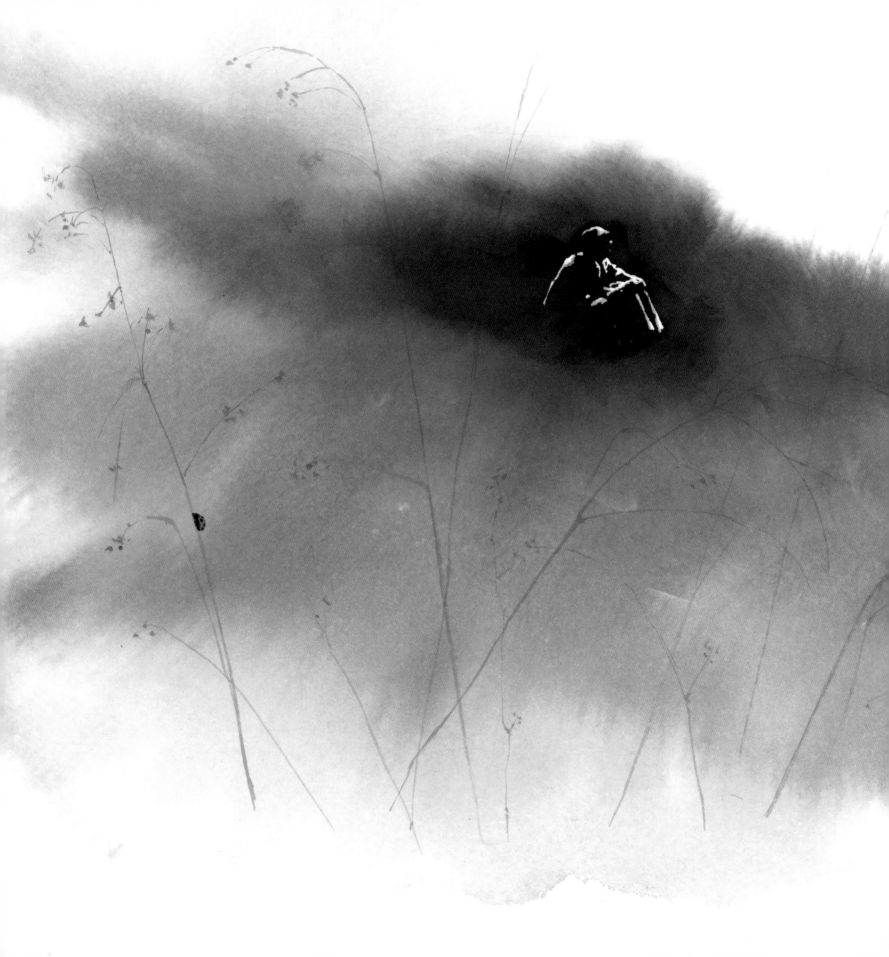

John watched for the butterflies every spring after that, and every spring, for a while, they came.

Twice more they asked for his help.

Twice more he was ready, and became a butterfly, and led them to safety.

Then, the year John turned seventeen, the flock stopped coming. His heart ached with questions. Had he grown too old? Had they simply forgotten him?

Or had something worse happened?

Whatever the reason, it was the most painful time of John's life. But he could never explain to his mother why he was so filled with despair, why he wept in his bed at night.

The next year John went to college, where he specialized in butterfly studies. Though his professors thought he was brilliant, he had a hard time in school — mostly because he could not bring himself to collect butterflies and pin them in display cases, as was expected of people in his profession. He preferred to study butterflies in the wild. In fact, the very sight of collections made him shudder.

Finally he was thrown out of the program.

He continued his work on his own.

Thirty years later it was John Farrington who persuaded the United States Congress to pass "The Butterfly Road" bill — a law setting aside a string of places to be kept forever wild and free so the monarchs could make their yearly migration in peace. Most researchers agreed it was John Farrington's law that saved the monarchs from extinction.

One day when John was a very old man, and his legs no longer worked, and he had not long left to live, the woman who cared for him pushed his wheelchair into the spring sunshine.

"Will you be all right here?" she asked, tucking a blanket around his legs. When John nodded, she returned to the house, leaving him to enjoy the warmth and the silence.

A few minutes after the nurse left, a cloud of butterflies settled around him. A thousand wings brushed his face, and the tiny scales fell all about him, fell on his eyes, his arms, his legs—his two legs, four legs, six legs...

His heart lifting with joy, John Farrington stretched his orange-and-black wings…and flew away forever.